W9-ALL-882

I
JOY
PD

Multiplying Madness!

Greg Dreamer thinks he's hit the jackpot when he's given a magic Halloween bag—a bag that multiplies everything he puts inside it.

Greg will definitely have more candy than anybody this Halloween—even more than that show-off Peter Boyd. He'll just make it in his magic bag! Mounds and mounds of it.

But Greg doesn't know his bag isn't just making candy—it's making mounds and mounds of trouble!

Also from R.L. Stine

The Beast®
The Beast® 2

Available from MINSTREL Books

For orders other than by individual consumers, Pocket Books grants a discount on the purchase of **10 or more** copies of single titles for special markets or premium use. For further details, please write to the Vice-President of Special Markets, Pocket Books, 1633 Broadway, New York, NY 10019-6785, 8th Floor.

For information on how individual consumers can place orders, please write to Mail Order Department, Simon & Schuster Inc., 200 Old Tappan Road, Old Tappan, NJ 07675.

HALLOWEEN BUGS ME!

A Parachute Press Book

A
MINSTREL®
BOOK

PUBLISHED BY POCKET BOOKS

New York London Toronto Sydney Tokyo Singapore

EAU CLAIRE DISTRICT LIBRARY

T 111449

The sale of this book without its cover is unauthorized. If you purchased this book without a cover, you should be aware that it was reported to the publisher as ''unsold and destroyed.'' Neither the author nor the publisher has received payment for the sale of this ''stripped book.''

This book is a work of fiction. Names, characters, places and incidents are products of the author's imagination or are used fictitiously. Any resemblance to actual events or locales or persons, living or dead, is entirely coincidental.

A MINSTREL PAPERBACK *Original*

A Minstrel Paperback published by
POCKET BOOKS, a division of Simon & Schuster Inc.
1230 Avenue of the Americas, New York, NY 10020

Copyright © 1997 by Parachute Press, Inc.

HALLOWEEN BUGS ME! WRITTEN BY BARBARA JOYCE

All rights reserved, including the right to reproduce this book or portions thereof in any form whatsoever. For information address Pocket Books, 1230 Avenue of the Americas, New York, NY 10020

ISBN: 0-671-00854-4

First Minstrel Books paperback printing October 1997

10 9 8 7 6 5 4 3 2 1

FEAR STREET is a registered trademark of Parachute Press, Inc.

A MINSTREL BOOK and colophon are registered trademarks of Simon & Schuster Inc.

Cover art by Broeck Steadman

Printed in the U.S.A.

EAU CLAIRE DISTRICT LIBRARY

R·L·STINE'S
GHOSTS of FEAR STREET®

HALLOWEEN BUGS ME!

Some kids are lucky.

Some aren't.

My name is Greg Dreamer. I'm smart. I'm a good athlete. And I'm a great drummer.

But I'm not lucky.

Don't get me wrong. I'm not complaining. Okay—maybe I am complaining.

But why can't *I* be lucky?

My friend Olivia is lucky.

Take today, for instance. Friday. Liv forgot to study for our math test. She was nervous. I could tell because she kept twirling her long brown braid around her fingers. That's what she does when she's nervous.

Anyway, we walked into class this morning and sat down at our desks. Liv was twirling away—when a substitute teacher walked into the room.

A substitute teacher! Can you believe it?

No math test.

That's lucky.

And that's what I was thinking as I walked home from school that afternoon and spotted Derek Boyd across the street.

Derek Boyd is the luckiest kid in the entire seventh grade. No—make that the luckiest kid in all of Shadyside Middle School.

Derek is always trying to prove he's better than me. He and I are always competing.

I have blond hair. But Derek's hair is blonder. I have blue eyes. But Derek's eyes are bluer.

I'm tall for my age—and strong. But Derek is taller and stronger. And he doesn't let me forget it.

Derek likes to compete. Derek likes to win. And he always does. *Always.* Like the last time we went on a class trip to the natural history museum. I found a quarter in the change return of the soda machine. Lucky, right?

But then I tried to buy a soda and the stupid machine ate all my money. Not just the quarter. All seventy cents.

Not so lucky.

And then Derek came along and bought a soda—

and the machine started spraying change at him like he hit the jackpot!

Now, that has to be luck. What else could it be?

If I were lucky, I could beat him. I know I could. That's what I was thinking when Derek walked over to me and burped in my ear. Really loud.

"Can you beat that, Dreamer?" He punched me in the arm. Really hard. I dropped my books on the sidewalk.

"Come on. I dare you. Try." He punched me again.

I glared at him. It was my I-mean-business look.

I took a deep breath. I gulped down some air.

I got ready to belch the loudest belch I could. This one would roar. I could feel it.

I opened my mouth—

"Hi, guys," Liv said. She tapped me on the back.

Broke my concentration.

I let out my burp.

It didn't quite roar.

"Got the hiccups again, Greg?" Liv asked.

"Ha! Hiccups! Good one!" Derek clapped me on the back. "Better luck next time."

Better luck next time. Yeah. Right.

"So—what are you going to be tonight?" Liv asked as I picked up my books.

It was Halloween. And I knew exactly what I was going to be. But I wasn't telling. I didn't want Derek to know. I didn't even want to give him a hint.

3

This Halloween I was finally going to beat Derek. This Halloween my costume was definitely going to be better than his.

"I'm not sure what I'm going to be," I lied.

"How about you, Liv?" Derek asked.

Liv hitched up her backpack. "My costume this year is totally great. I'm going as a mummy."

"Didn't you go as a mummy last year?" I asked.

"Yes. That's what's so great about it!" she exclaimed. "My costume is still in perfect condition. I don't have to waste time making a new one."

Liv is very into being practical.

Derek shrugged. "Well, I have a new costume, and it's awesome! It will definitely beat yours, Dreamer!" He punched me in the arm again. Then he took off down the block.

"He even runs faster than I do," I said, disgusted. "He beats me at everything."

"All this competing with Derek is crazy," Liv complained as we headed home. "Why do you do it?"

"Because I have to beat Derek at something," I told her. "I have to. Just once, I have to win."

Liv's house is on the same block as mine. The whole way home she went on and on about how stupid it was to compete.

"Stupid and crazy and sick. Stupid and crazy and sick," she said over and over again. "Stupid and crazy and—Uh-oh."

"Huh?"

"Uh-oh," Liv repeated. "Here comes Muffin."

I groaned. Muffin is Mrs. O'Connor's dog. My dad says Mrs. O'Connor is a nut. I don't know about that, but *Muffin* is definitely crazy. He's just a little Scottish terrier, but he thinks he's a Doberman.

The dog charged down the block, heading straight for us. *"Arf! Arf! Grrrf!"* he yapped.

"No!" I shouted as Muffin lunged for my right foot. He grabbed my shoelaces in his mouth. He tossed his head madly back and forth, tugging at them.

"Stop!" I ordered. But he just tugged harder, untying them. Chewing them to bits with his sharp teeth.

I handed my books to Liv. I pried Muffin's mouth open and freed my laces.

He growled—then sank his teeth into my other sneaker.

I knew from experience that Muffin wasn't going to quit. There was only one thing to do. "Come on!" I yelled to Liv. I started to run, dragging the dumb dog with me.

I dragged Muffin past two houses. Finally he had to let go. But then he chased me all the way to my front yard.

Liv and I leaped over my gate. We ran inside the house. I slammed the door behind us and collapsed on the hall floor.

"Greg, is that you?" Mom came out of the kitchen. She stared down at me. "Why are you sitting on the floor?"

"Because he's lazy," my six-year-old sister, Raina, piped up. She followed Mom out of the kitchen.

Liv choked back a laugh.

"Maybe you're right, honey." Mom ran her hand through Raina's curly blond hair. "Greg, you need exercise. Go up and clean your room. My book discussion group is coming tomorrow."

My mom is funny that way. I mean, why clean my room for her reading group? It's not like they're going to meet in *there*.

But try pointing that out to my mom.

"I'll clean it later, Mom. I want to show Liv something first."

"Greg, your room has to be clean before dinner. Otherwise . . . no trick-or-treating tonight," Mom warned.

"Okay, okay," I grumbled under my breath.

"What do you want to show me?" Liv asked as we headed up the stairs.

"You'll see."

"See what?" Raina asked, following us.

"Get lost," I told her.

"Greg! Don't talk to Raina that way," Mom yelled up the steps. "You're lucky to have a little sister who loves you."

Yeah. Lucky. Right.

Raina followed us right into my bedroom. She sat down on my rug. Our cat sauntered into the room and sat in her lap.

It was supposed to be *my* cat. I begged my mom and dad for it for months and months. "Raina has a hamster. Why can't I have a pet too?" I pleaded.

I knew just what I wanted. A mysterious, coal-black cat with deep green eyes. I'd seen him in the pet store.

My parents finally gave in and bought me a cat for my birthday. But they took *Raina* to the pet store with them. She got to pick out the cat. *And* name it.

I stared down at the cat.

Our sweet, small, white, fluffy cat with pale blue eyes.

Let me tell you something. A twelve-year-old guy should *not* have a sweet, small, white, fluffy cat. It's embarrassing.

Let me tell you something else. A twelve-year-old guy *definitely*—I repeat, *definitely*—should *not* have a cat named Princess.

"Boy, Princess really grew." Liv bent down to pet her.

"Yeah. But she's not as big as Derek's cat," I grumbled.

After we got Princess, Derek got a cat too. A really big cat. Coal-black with green eyes.

My cat.

"Greg, this dumb competition has got to end! It doesn't matter who has a bigger cat!" Liv shouted.

"It does matter!" I yelled back. "Derek always wins. But that's going to change. It's going to change today!"

"Today? Why today?" Liv asked.

"Because today is Halloween. And I'm going to show Derek this year who is best," I told her.

"And how are you going to do that?" Liv folded her arms.

"Simple," I answered. "I have a plan."

2

"**A**re you ready?" I called from inside my closet.

"I've been ready for the last ten minutes," Liv answered. "What are you doing in there?"

"You'll see. Just give me a few more seconds. It's all part of my plan," I said.

Then I leaped out of the closet—and Raina and Liv shrieked in terror.

"Wow! That's a great costume!" Liv reached out a hand and touched it. "Ewww. It's so . . . hairy."

"I know. Isn't it awesome?" I studied my costume in the mirror. My totally gruesome werewolf costume.

It was very hairy. Very thick and very hairy.

I had worked hard on that costume. I'd made it really gross. In some spots the fur was matted down and sticky with a mixture of maple syrup and vegetable oil.

Dead bugs nested in the fur. Flies, worms—even a big, hairy spider. I must have spent two hours gluing them all in place. They were fake, but they looked pretty real.

"What's that?" Raina reached out. She touched a bloated worm clinging to the moist hair. "Oh, yuck!" She drew her hand back quickly. "It feels wet."

"Want to see something totally gross?" I asked.

I turned to show them the scab on the right side of the wolf mask. It looked like a fresh cut from a wolf fight. It had fake pus dripping from it and everything. It cost a lot extra. But I had to have it!

"It's a great costume, Greg." Liv couldn't stop staring at it. "It really is."

"I know." I took off the mask and smiled. "Derek is going to have to go pretty far to beat this. He's going to need more than a costume to beat *me* tonight. He's going to need a miracle!"

Liv sighed. Then she headed for the door.

"Hey! Where are you going? I'm not finished telling you the rest of my plan!"

She stopped in the doorway. "I'm going home. I think I've heard enough."

"Wait a second. Look!" I reached into my closet and pulled out a huge orange plastic trick-or-treat bag.

"Can you believe the size of this thing?" I asked her.

"It's ridiculous. It's as big as a suitcase!" Liv shook her head.

"I know. And tonight I'm going to fill it completely. I'm going to get twice as much candy as Derek!"

Liv started down the steps.

"Tonight is the night, Liv!" I called after her. "Tonight I am going to beat Derek. I'll have the best costume *and* the most candy!"

"Whatever," I heard Liz call. Then the front door slammed.

"Raina! Greg!" Mom called. "Come on down. Time for dinner."

"Will you give me some of your Halloween candy later?" Raina asked as we made our way downstairs.

"No way!" I scoffed.

"Then I'm telling Mom—" she started to whine.

"Mom won't care," I cut her off. "She doesn't want you to eat candy."

"I'm telling Mom," Raina started again, "that you didn't clean your room."

After dinner, I cleaned my room.

Then I went out to meet Liv.

In the light of the full moon, she was easy to spot. She was the only mummy wearing short-sleeved bandages.

"I forgot to check the sleeves," she said miserably. "My arms must have grown."

We walked a few steps. Then Liv stopped. She tried to tug her bandages down to her wrists.

I scanned the street, searching for Derek. Our block looks totally creepy tonight, I thought. Jack-o'-lanterns sat on almost every porch. Flickering candles inside them lit up their eerie grins and cast an orange glow over the houses.

A chilly breeze began to blow.

Something clattered behind us.

I spun around—and gasped. A skeleton hung from one of the branches. Its bones rattled in the wind.

The wind picked up. It howled through the trees. Leaves swirled at our feet.

I heard the distant laughter of some kids on the corner. But there was no sign of Derek.

We walked toward Mrs. O'Connor's house.

Liv stopped and tugged on her bandages some more.

"You look great. Really, Liv. Come on." I urged. "I want to find Derek. I can't wait to show him my costume. I can't wait to see his face."

We walked some more.

I heard rustling behind the tall bushes that lined the street.

I stopped and glanced around.

No one there.

We took a few more steps.

This time Liv heard the rustling too. Our eyes darted to the shrubs. We saw them quiver in the moonlight.

"Is someone following us?" Liv's voice shook.

"I—I think so," I whispered. "Walk faster."

We broke into a jog—and heard footsteps.

We started to run.

The footsteps grew louder. Closer.

The bushes to my left quaked, and a dark creature sprang out from them.

It was big. And hairy.

In the glow of the moon, I could see its red, burning eyes and its slack jaw gleaming with spittle.

"A werewolf!" I cried. "A real werewolf! Run, Liv!"

Before I could move, the werewolf let out a shuddering howl and leaped through the air!

EAU CLAIRE DISTRICT LIBRARY

3

The werewolf landed hard against my chest. Even through my mask I could smell its damp animal smell.

With its chest right against mine, it wrapped its heavy arms around me, locking my arms close to my sides. It bellowed a loud, deep growl.

I pushed my arms out. Hard. With a heave, I freed myself.

"Run, Liv! *Run!*" I cried again.

My heart pounding, I tore down the block.

"Did you see it?" I asked Liv, panting. "Did you see the werewolf? I—I think it had two heads!"

Liv didn't answer me.

I risked a glance to my right. Then my left.

Liv was nowhere in sight.

It's got her! I realized. *I have to go back! I have to help her!*

I spun around—and froze.

Liv stood right where I had left her—right next to the werewolf.

She stared at me for a second.

Then she burst into laughter.

"Oh no," I moaned. "It can't be. It just can't be!"

I made my way slowly back to Liv. I felt sick.

"You can run pretty fast—when you're scared to death!" the werewolf remarked. It took off one of its heads.

That's right. It was Derek—in a werewolf costume as gross as mine.

No—it was grosser.

The eyes on his mask glowed. And the fur was thicker. It even *smelled* like wolf fur.

The fake drool was really disgusting. And the costume had *two* heads. Two hideous heads.

"Not a bad costume." Derek ran his paw over my fur. "Like the bugs. Nice touch. But . . . I win!"

Now I was really steamed.

"See you." Derek started to leave. "It's time for me to collect more candy than you."

"No way!" I sputtered. *"I'm* the one who is going to collect the most candy. Look at this!" I held up my giant trick-or-treat bag. "There's no way I can loose with this."

"Whoa!" Derek stopped. His eyes opened wide. "That's a big bag!"

Then he grinned. "But it's not as big as mine!"

Derek held up his trick-or-treat bag. It was enormous. *Twice* the size of my bag.

My eyes narrowed. "I'll fill my bag up—and another and another!" I shouted.

"Dream on, Dreamer!" he hooted. "I'm going to win—because I always do!"

"Stop it!" Liv yelled. "Stop it, right now! This is sick. Who cares about stupid Halloween candy! Who cares about winning?"

"Gotta go." Grinning, Derek took off down the street.

"Come on, Liv." I tugged on her bandages, dragging her in the opposite direction from Derek. "We can't waste any time."

I charged blindly up to house after house. "Trick or treat!" I yelled as soon as anybody opened their door.

The second they dropped the candy in my bag, I was off, racing to the next house.

"Slow down," Liv complained.

"We can't slow down!" I panted. "We need more candy! Lots more candy!"

"Trick or treat! Trick or treat!"

I raced through the streets.

I think I rang nearly every doorbell in Shadyside. I collected candy. A lot of candy.

But it wasn't enough. When I glanced inside my bag, it was only half filled.

"Hurry, Liv! We need more!" I ran ahead and turned down the next block.

"Greg!" she cried. *"Stop!"*

I waited impatiently for her to catch up. "What's the matter?"

"Are you crazy? We can't trick-or-treat on this street!" she exclaimed.

"Why not?" I asked.

"Why not! You've totally lost it, Greg. Didn't you even notice where we are?" Liv pointed to the street sign. "We cannot trick-or-treat here. This is *Fear Street!*"

Fear Street.

I shivered in the cool October air.

Liv and I never walk down Fear Street. Never.

Too many weird things happen on this street. At least, that's what I've heard. I don't know whether to believe the stories or not, but Liv definitely does.

Liv says most of the houses on Fear Street are haunted. And horrible things happen in the ones that aren't.

She says she once met a kid who was trapped in the Fear Street Cemetery. Trapped by a ghost who wanted him to stay there. Forever.

And the Fear Street Woods—I shivered again just thinking about those woods. No birds live in the Fear Street Woods. None at all. And no one knows why.

Maybe Liv was right. Maybe we shouldn't . . .

No! We should!

Of course we should!

"Liv, we have to trick-or-treat on Fear Street!" I gripped her wrist. "Come on. It's perfect! Derek will never even think of trick-or-treating here! We'll clean up! We'll definitely get more candy than he will!"

Liv shook her head.

"Please, Liv? Just walk down the street with me. Please?"

"Oh, all right," she said at last.

I guided Liv down Fear Street. I walked slowly—because it was *really* dark. The streetlights are always out on Fear Street.

"We won't go to all the houses. Just a few. Nothing will happen to us. You'll see," I declared.

I sounded pretty convincing, I thought.

But as I gazed around, I started to change my mind.

Fear Street was definitely creepy.

The trees on our street were bright with red and yellow fall leaves. But the trees here were bare.

I gazed up at their branches. They grew thick and twisted tightly together. They hung low over our heads, blocking out even the slightest ray of moonlight.

The houses were even creepier.

They rose up high and sprawled out over the winding street. With their cold stone and brick, they sat dark and dreary. No colorful trim painted on the shutters. No cheerful welcome mats in front of the doors.

Rolling lawns stretched out in front of some of the houses—gardens of overgrown crabgrass, dotted with bald and blackened spots.

A high fence of rusted black iron ran next to the sidewalk. It was tipped with sharp spikes.

Another shiver ran through me.

Liv stared around and shivered too.

"I have a bad feeling about this, Greg," she murmured. She walked close to me.

"Everything is going to be fine," I told her as the wind began to gust.

"I don't think so." Liv reached for her braid. But it was tucked into her mummy costume. So she just grabbed a piece of bandage and started twisting that.

"Something is going to happen to us here," she said fearfully. "Something terrible. I just know it."

4

We stopped in front of a house near the end of Fear Street. A three-story house—a mansion, really.

I counted the windows. There were eight on each floor. Twenty-four windows! And that was just in the front.

Twenty-four windows—all totally dark. Not a glimmer of light peeked through. No lamp glow. No flicker from a TV or fireplace.

"Let's keep going," Liv said. "Nobody's home."

"Somebody might be home." I started up the dark path. "It's a big house. Maybe they're in the back."

Liv and I stepped up on the front porch. The old wood creaked under our weight. We stopped.

"Are you sure you want to do this?" Liv looped her loose bandages into a knot around her fingers.

I glanced up at the house. At the rotting shutters that dangled from the black windows. At the soot that caked the stone walls.

I wasn't sure at all.

I glanced up and down the block.

All the houses on Fear Street looked kind of spooky.

Might as well start with this one, I thought. *We have to start somewhere—and I have to get more candy than Derek!*

"We'll ring the bell, get our candy, and leave— fast," I promised.

I rang the bell.

We waited for someone to answer.

"Nobody's home. Let's go." Liv started to tug me down the steps. Then we heard the squeaky doorknob turn.

I turned around. The door opened a crack.

"Hello?" I called.

A green, scaly hand shot out from the dark and grabbed my wrist!

"Hey! Help! Let me go!" I yelled. I tried to jerk free, but the hand held on tightly.

"Let him go!" Liv smacked the hand hard.

We heard a cry inside.

A second later the hand released me . . . and the door swung open.

"Sorry." A boy stood in the doorway. He seemed about my age, but very thin, almost frail. His stringy dark hair hung in his eyes.

In his hand he held a fake monster claw. He waved it at us. "I was just trying to have some fun. It's Halloween, you know."

"Um, we know," I said. "We're trick-or-treating."

"Great," the boy said. "Come in. I'll give you some candy." He turned, motioning for us to follow.

"I am *not* going in there," Liv whispered to me.

"Come on. We'll go in for a second. We'll just get our candy and leave," I pleaded.

Liv rolled her eyes. But she followed me through the door.

We stepped inside. We stood in a large living room—in the glow of hundreds of flickering candles.

There were candles *everywhere*. On the antique tables and wooden bookcases. On an old trunk. On the fireplace mantel. Even on the floor. The whole room smelled of hot wax.

Creepy!

My eyes darted to the windows. They were draped with curtains. Heavy black curtains that blocked out all the light. No wonder the house had seemed deserted from outside.

"Let's get out of here!" Liv whispered.

"Okay. Okay. As soon as he gives us our candy." I stared around the room some more. I'd never seen anything like it.

Crystals were grouped around every candle. Pink and purple crystals, glowing in the candlelight.

But the creepiest thing of all were the clocks. Clocks on the tables. Clocks on the bookcases. Clocks on the walls.

All ticking. Ticking. Ticking.

So many clocks.

The boy with the claw just stood there in the middle of the room, staring at us. I wondered if maybe he forgot about our candy.

"Do you, um, go to Shadyside Middle School?" Liv tried to make conversation with him.

"No. I go to a private school," he answered in a raspy voice. "My name is Ricky. I have a sore throat."

I studied Ricky's face. His skin was pale—so pale I could see the blue veins underneath.

"What are your names?" he croaked.

"I'm Liv." Liv shot me a let's-go-now look from the corner of her eye.

"My name is Greg—and I'm kind of in a hurry," I told Ricky. "See, I'm trying to get more candy than a friend of mine."

"I think I can help you," a sharp voice behind me replied.

I spun around and stared into the speckled gray eyes of an old woman.

She wore a black velvet shirt and a long skirt. Gold bracelets jangled from her bony wrists.

She was short and thin—as thin as Ricky. Her gray hair hung in wisps around her face. Her skin was lined with deep, deep wrinkles.

Everything about her seemed old—except her voice. Her voice was strong and clear.

The old woman walked up to me. She moved briskly. Not like an old woman at all.

She snatched my trick-or-treat bag from my grasp.

"Hey! Where are you going with that?" I asked, surprised. But she left the room without a word.

Ricky sat down on a shredded couch. He sat and stared at us. Just stared.

The place was really giving me the creeps.

"Greg, I want to go—" Liv began. Then she broke off and gasped. "Look!"

I followed her gaze to a shadowy corner of the room—where two large, glowing eyes peered at us.

I took a sharp breath.

I stared into those glowing yellow eyes.

Then I realized. "It's just an owl," I said, relieved. "An owl sitting on top of a grandfather clock."

"I thought owls were supposed to be smart. This one must be pretty stupid to hang around here," Liz muttered.

I laughed. "It's dumber than you think, Liv. It's stuffed."

"I want to go *now!*" Liv was twisting her bandage around her fingers like crazy.

I wanted to go too, to be honest. Not only did this house give me the creeps, I was also starting to sweat inside my werewolf costume. "Okay. If the old lady doesn't come back in a minute, we'll—"

"Shhh," Liv interrupted me. "Do you hear that?"

I listened.

I heard chanting.

Low chanting. Coming from another room.

I listened closely. It was the weird old woman's voice. But I couldn't make out the words. She was speaking in some foreign language. A language I'd never even heard before.

"What is she doing?" I asked Ricky.

Ricky didn't answer. He just stared at me.

He was making me nervous. Why didn't he talk? I stepped over to an antique table and picked up an old leather book that was resting there.

"Whoa," I whispered when I read the title. Silently I pointed it out to Liv.

In worn gold lettering it said: *Magic.*

"That's it. I'm out of here." Liz headed for the door. I was right on her heels.

And then, all of a sudden, the old lady stood in front of us. Between us and the door.

How did she get there?

"Going so soon?" she asked. "You can't leave without this." She handed me a big orange cloth bag with a jack-o'-lantern stitched on the front.

"Hey! This isn't my bag! This is a different bag!"

I glanced inside. My candy! I'd swear some of it was missing. The pile definitely looked smaller than before.

What did this weird old lady do with my bag? And my candy?

I handed the bag back to the old woman. "I want *my* bag!"

"Take this one." The old woman shoved the bag into my hand. "Take it—and don't worry about it. You'll have more candy than your friend. Then you'll come back and thank me—won't you?"

A small smile spread across her lips—and every clock in the house began to gong.

The room thundered with the sound of the clocks—gonging, chiming, ringing, bonging.

Liv covered her ears and ran to the door.

I took the bag.

But I was never coming back, I could tell you that.

The old woman opened the door. We ran out and sprinted down the steps. Liv raced down Fear Street.

"Wait up!" I yelled. "We can't go home yet. That old lady stole my candy! We have to collect more! Otherwise I won't win!"

"It's too late," Liv shouted. "It's ten o'clock. It's too late for trick-or-treating."

Liv was right. It was too late.

I glanced down and spotted a Tootsie Roll on the ground. I tossed it into my bag.

Whoa. Big deal. A whole night of trick-or-treating—and my bag wasn't even half filled.

Liv and I walked slowly to my house. There was Derek, pacing back and forth on my porch. "Okay, Dreamer," he called as I plodded up the front steps. "It's time to crown the trick-or-treat champ!"

"Yeah, yeah," I mumbled.

Give up, I told myself as we headed inside. *Face it—you're just not lucky.*

Up in my bedroom, Derek lifted his bag high over my bed.

He tilted it slowly—and a mountain of candy spilled out.

"Your turn!" He grinned.

I gripped the bottom of my bag.

I turned it over.

I spilled it out—and gasped in shock.

5

Candy!

Tons of candy.

Streaming out of my bag. Showering down on my bed.

Snickers bars. Candy corn. Milky Ways. M&M's. Bubble gum. Lollipops. Tootsie Rolls. Reese's Pieces.

At least ten of each kind!

Tons and tons of candy!

Much more than Derek!

"You said your bag was practically empty!" Liv stared in amazement at the mountain of treats on the bed.

"It—It was," I stammered.

"I *lost?*" Derek said in disbelief. He glared at me.

A grin spread across my face. *Yes!*

"I won! I did it! I won!" I pumped my fist in the air. "I told you I'd beat you!" I whacked Derek on the back.

Derek crumpled his trick-or-treat bag into a tight ball. He threw it on the floor. He stormed out of my room. We heard his footsteps pound down the stairs.

"I won! I won! I won!" I cheered. "I finally won!"

"I don't have anywhere near this much! Greg—how *did* you get so much candy?" Liv sifted her hands through the huge pile.

I stared down at it. "I don't know," I admitted.

Princess darted into my room just then and leaped into my pile of candy. Raina ran into my room, chasing after her.

"Wow!" Raina eyed my bed. She plunged her hands down to the bottom of the pile. Then she brought them up fast, flinging candy everywhere.

I scowled at her. "Get out of my room, Raina!"

"Make me." Raina sat down. She grabbed a candy bar, ripped off the wrapper, and took a big bite.

"Who said you could have that?" I snatched the candy bar from her.

"I don't want your stupid candy anyway." Raina jumped up and marched out of my room. "It stinks."

Liv stared at the pile of Halloween loot, shaking her head.

"I just don't get it." She took the trick-or-treat bag

from me and stared inside. "Where did all that candy come from?"

She turned the bag over and over in her hands. She examined it from every angle.

I watched her. At last I cleared my throat.

"Are you thinking what I'm thinking?" I asked.

Slowly, Liv nodded.

"The bag must be magic," she declared. "There's no other explanation."

I took a deep breath. I picked up a Snickers bar and tossed it into the trick-or-treat bag.

I held the bag closed for a few seconds.

Then I opened it and peeked inside.

"Wow!" I cried. "Ten! There are *ten* Snickers bars in here!" I spilled them out for Liv to see.

Liv's eyes practically popped out of her head.

We both stared at the bag in silence.

It was unbelievable.

Liv handed the bag back to me. She unwrapped one of the candy bars and took a bite. Then she wrinkled her nose. "You know, Raina's right."

"Huh? About what?"

"This candy stinks. It tastes funny."

I took a bite from her candy bar. "No it doesn't. It tastes fine to me."

I sat down on my bed. I studied the bag. "That old lady must have put some kind of spell on it. This is so cool! Let's try something else!"

I lifted my glass baseball trophy off my desk.

No. I changed my mind. I wasn't sure what the bag would do, and I didn't want anything to happen to my trophy.

I grabbed my baseball instead.

I tossed it into the bag.

I closed the bag. I waited a few seconds, then turned it over.

Ten baseballs came rolling out!

Then I threw in my limited-edition Superman comic.

Ten comics came out. *Ten!*

"I have ten limited-edition Superman comics!" I shouted.

"Greg!" Liv gasped. "You're going to be rich!"

"I know! These are worth a fortune!" I fanned the valuable comics in my hand.

"That's not what I mean!" Liv's eyes lit with excitement. She dug into her pocket and came up with a ten-dollar bill.

"Put it in the bag!" she said. "Let's see if it works!"

6

I placed the ten-dollar bill in the bag. I closed the bag.

Then I closed my eyes and prayed. *Please work! Please work!*

"Give me that!" Liv grabbed the bag and peered inside.

"Well? Did it work?" I demanded. "Did it?"

"Yes!" Liv shrieked. "It worked! It worked!"

She turned the bag upside down. *Ten* ten-dollar bills showered down on us.

One hundred dollars!

"I'm rich! I'm rich!" I cried.

Liv picked up the money from the floor. She stared at it. "No—no, you're not rich," she said.

"Wh-what do you mean?" I stammered.

"I'm rich!" she shouted. "That was my money! I'm rich!"

"Ha-ha. You're a riot." I reached into the top drawer of my night table and pulled out a twenty-dollar bill. I was saving it for new drumsticks. But this was an emergency.

I put it in the bag. Closed the bag. Turned it upside down.

Two hundred dollars came out!

Liv and I stared at our money.

"We have *three hundred dollars!*" she gasped.

"It's amazing!" I cried. "Wait until I tell Mom and Dad about this bag. Hey, Mom!" I started toward my door.

"Wait!" Liv jumped up and clapped her hand over my mouth. "You can't do that!" she declared. "They'll take the bag away from you. They'll make you turn it in to the police or something!"

Whoa. I never thought of that. Good thing Liv was around!

I pried her hand away from my mouth. "You're right," I agreed. "We better keep it a secret."

"Great." Liv stacked our money into a neat pile. "Let's go to the Division Street Mall tomorrow. Let's go shopping!"

Saturday morning I got up early.

I couldn't wait to go to the mall!

I got dressed really fast.

Raina popped into my room as I was tying my sneakers. "Where are you going?"

"To the mall with Liv," I told her.

"I want to go too," Raina said.

"No way!"

"If you don't take me, I'll rip up all your comic books when you're gone." Raina grabbed my ten limited-edition comics from my desk.

"Give those back!" I yanked them from her and tossed them behind me on the bed.

Raina pointed to the bed and laughed.

Princess sat there, batting the pages with her paw.

I rolled my eyes. "Take Princess and go," I ordered, handing the cat to Raina. "And I'm warning you— stay out of my room!"

Raina left and I finished getting dressed. I hid my comics under some clothes on the top shelf of my closet—just in case.

Then I raced over to Liv's. We hurried to the Division Street Mall.

"I want to go to Music World first," Liv said as we walked into the mall.

So that's where we headed. And wouldn't you know it? The first person we bumped into was Derek.

"Hey, Derek! I bet I can buy more CDs than you!" I declared.

"Forget about betting, Greg!" Liv said. "You already won last night. Don't start acting stupid again." She sounded irritated.

"It's too late." Derek laughed. "Greg is already stupid—he forgot that I always have more money than he does. Always!"

He reached into his wallet and took out two twenties and a ten. Fifty dollars. He fanned it in front of my face. "Beat that, Dreamer."

I reached into my windbreaker pocket and waved my money in front of him—my two hundred dollars.

Derek turned pale.

"This isn't over!" he shouted.

Then he stomped out of the store.

"What a sore loser!" I laughed.

"Come on already." Liv tugged me over to the CD rack.

We picked out fifteen CDs. The store was crowded, so it took a while to pay for them. But I didn't care. I was rich! Nothing could spoil my mood.

"Where do you want to go next?" Liv asked as we reached the door.

"How about—" I began.

A wailing alarm pierced the air.

A tall, beefy security guard stepped in front of us. Right in front of the door.

"You two!" he barked, glaring at us. "Stop right there!"

7

The guard grabbed our arms and pulled us toward the back of the store. His fingers were clamped firmly around my bicep.

"What's going on? Wh-Where are we going?" I stammered.

"To the police," he said gruffly.

"The police!" Liv gasped. "Why? We didn't do anything wrong!"

"That's what they all say," the guard grumbled.

"What did we do?" Liv wailed. "Are you going to send us to jail?"

The guard didn't answer.

He marched us through the aisles.

Oh no! We are *going to jail,* I thought. *We're going to jail—and I don't even know why!*

As we stumbled through the crowded store, the other shoppers gawked at us. They shook their heads and frowned. They shrank back from us.

"Here they are." The guard delivered us to a short, chubby man with round cheeks and a black mustache. His Music World name tag read MANAGER.

A few wisps of black hair fell over his forehead. Except for those wisps, he was bald. A pair of reading glasses perched on the tip of his nose. He peered over their tops, shifting his gaze from me to Liv.

"Where did you get this?" he asked, holding up a handful of tens and twenties. I guessed they must be the bills we used to pay for the CDs.

I shot a glance at Liv.

Her face was pale. She twisted her braid around her fingers.

"Well?" the manager demanded.

"We, um, found it," I murmured.

The manager studied my face for a moment. Then he studied the bills in his hand. "They're counterfeit," he finally said. "They're not real."

"No way! That can't be!" I exclaimed.

"They're not real," he repeated. "Feel this." He held out one of my twenty-dollar bills. I rubbed my fingers over it.

Then he reached into his pocket and took out another twenty-dollar bill. "Now touch this one," he ordered.

I touched it.

"It feels different!" I gasped. My fingers started to tremble.

The manager fanned my money in his palm. "Bad counterfeits," he said. "More like play money."

My heart pounded in my chest.

Oh no! We are *going to jail!*

The manager took a step back from us. "You look like nice kids. I've seen you in the store before. Now tell me the truth. Did you really *find* this money?" He narrowed his eyes at me.

"Yes. We really did," I answered. "Honest."

Well, it was as close to the truth as I was going to get. No way was I going to try to explain about the magic bag!

"Okay. Give me back the CDs," the manager told me.

My hands shook as I gave him the bag.

"I'm going to let you go—this time. But there had better not be a next time," he said sternly.

I gulped. "Yes sir. I mean, no sir. I mean—"

"Come on," Liv broke in.

We left the store as quickly as we could. Liv was shaking so much, we headed for a bench so she could sit down.

"I don't believe that!" Her voice quivered.

Then she jumped up from the bench.

"This is all your fault!" she shouted.

"My fault?" I glared at her. "You were the one who wanted to put money in the bag in the first place! How is it my fault?"

"Because I *told* you something was wrong with that candy! I *told* you it didn't taste right! And now something is wrong with the money too."

Liv pulled out her fake money and tore it up.

"Well, that's not my fault," I declared. "It's the bag's fault! How was I supposed to know it didn't make perfect copies? How was I supposed to know the copies were a little, well, off?"

"I told you," Liv insisted.

We argued about whose fault it was all the way to my house.

We argued about it all the way up to my room.

We were still arguing about it as we walked through my bedroom doorway.

And then we stopped arguing about it—when we saw Raina in my room. Sitting on my bed.

With the trick-or-treat bag in her lap.

She was reaching inside it. With something in her hand.

"Don't, Raina!" I screamed. "Don't put *that* in the bag!"

8

Raina plunged her hand deeper into the bag.

"No! *Stop!*" I leaped across the room. "Don't put the hamster in there!"

I grabbed Raina's wrist. I jerked it out of the bag, hard.

Her hand came out—with the hamster sitting in her palm.

"That was a close one." I let out a sigh.

"Ow! You're hurting me! Let go." Raina wrenched free of my grip.

I snatched the bag away from her. "I told you to stay out of here!" I yelled, tossing the bag across the room.

"Greg! Look!" Liv screamed. She stared across the room in horror.

I followed her gaze—and screamed too.

Princess was crawling inside the bag.

"Princess, *no!* Get out of there!" I dove for the bag. Too late.

She was completely inside it.

I tried to grab the bag, but I couldn't.

It leaped around on the floor. It jerked wildly from side to side. Snarls and hisses filled the air.

"Wow!" Raina stared wide-eyed. "It looks like Princess is fighting another cat in there!"

I really hoped she was wrong.

Finally I pounced on the bag. I lay on top of it. It jerked and twitched for a second. Then it stopped.

My heart pounded as I sat up and let go.

Princess scrambled out.

Followed by another Princess.

And another Princess. And another. And another. And another.

"Oh *noooo!*" I moaned.

I watched in horror as ten white cats filled my room. One jumped on my desk and pawed at my glass baseball trophy.

It started to topple.

"Greg!" Liv screamed. "Get it!"

I leaped across the room—and caught the trophy

before it fell. "Whew! That was close!" I said, holding it up.

"Not that!" she hollered. "The bag!"

I whirled around—and saw two cats crawl back into the bag. The bag jerked and hopped across the room. It was totally out of control!

The second I wrestled it to the ground, twenty more cats scrambled out!

"Oh nooooo," I moaned.

Now I had almost *thirty* cats in my small room.

Cats creeping on my desk, stretching on my bed, tiptoeing along on my bookshelves, padding across my drum set.

Every inch of carpet was covered with cats. So many they couldn't walk without bumping into each other.

They swarmed around my ankles, meowing.

I tried to move away, but I couldn't. There was no place to go without stepping on a cat.

"Wow!" Raina's eyes opened wide in amazement. "You're in trouble now, Greg!"

"Get them!" I yelled.

Liv and I ran around the room, trying to gather up the cats. I scooped one up—and it let out a long, menacing hiss.

"Ow!" Liv screamed as another cat sank its teeth into her ankle.

I picked up a third cat.

42

I cuddled it in my arms. "Nice kitty," I murmured. "Nice Princess."

The cat gave a long, throaty purr—then swiped its claws across my cheek.

"Ow!" I dropped the cat and ran my hand over my cheek.

Blood! There was blood trickling from my raw skin!

"Watch out, Greg! Behind you!" Liv yelled.

I whirled around—just in time to dodge a cat leaping from the dresser. It was aiming for my head, but it landed on my leg. Clung to it. Sank its sharp claws into my shin.

Another cat flew at me. It landed on my chest. I jerked my head back as it tried to scratch my eyes out.

"These cats aren't like Princess," Raina whimpered. She shrank back as two hissing cats moved in on her. "These cats are mean. I'm going back to my room." Cradling her hamster in her hands, she darted out.

The terrifying cats tore at my bedspread. My curtains. My carpet. They batted my books off the shelves. They ripped my homework to shreds. They chewed through my pillow.

"There's something wrong with these cats!" I cried. "They're vicious! It's the bag's fault! They're *not* like Princess! The bag changed them!"

Liv backed herself against a wall. "This isn't working," she shouted. "We can't pick up these cats!"

I shielded my face with my hands as another cat hurled itself at me.

"What else can we do?" I wailed. "We have to get rid of them. We can't just leave them here! Do you have a better idea?"

Liv peeled a cat off her leg and gazed at me with narrowed eyes. "Yes, I do," she said. "I have an idea— but you're not going to like it."

9

"**M**uffin? Use Muffin to get rid of the cats! No way!" I declared.

We were standing in the hall outside my room. Inside, nearly thirty cats yowled and scratched at the door. Liv had grabbed the bag while I cleared a path to the door.

"It's the *only* way," Liv insisted. "The way to get rid of cats is with dogs. The dogs will chase the cats out! If you have a better idea, let's hear it!"

I didn't have a better idea—so we sneaked out of my house and over to Mrs. O'Connor's yard.

Muffin was lying on the walkway. The second he caught sight of us he let out a growl. His lip curled back to bare his teeth.

"I don't like this," I muttered, staring at the crazy dog. Muffin was little, but he was mean.

"We have no choice," Liv reminded me. "Do you remember the plan?"

I nodded. The plan. That's what had me worried.

Liv marched up to Muffin.

He trained his eyes on her. Watching her. Waiting to see what she was up to.

I tiptoed up behind him—and threw the trick-or-treat bag over him.

"Arf! Grff! Rowf!" Inside the bag, Muffin erupted in furious barks and snarls.

"Got him!" I cried. "Let's go!"

Liv helped me scoop the bag up.

I held it closed, but it wasn't easy. Muffin struggled like a maniac.

We started back to my house. Liv held up the bottom of the bag. I clutched the top. Muffin barked madly.

"Hurry! Run. Before Mrs. O'Connor hears him!" Liv grunted.

Mom and Dad were in the living room, near the front door, so we had to sneak in through the back.

"What's all that noise?" Mom called to us as we struggled up the steps with the bag.

"Just a new CD Liv's playing on her boom box," I answered, gasping for breath. "Sorry. We'll lower the volume."

We reached my bedroom. I threw open the door.

We dropped the bag on the floor—and ten furious Muffins burst out of the bag.

Luckily for us, the dogs forgot all about us the moment they spotted the cats. The dogs eyed their prey in menacing silence.

The cats returned their gaze. Their fur bristled. They arched their backs.

I hope this works, I prayed. *It's got to work. It's just got to!*

The dogs curled back their lips.

They bared their fangs.

They opened their jaws—

And *quacked!*

10

Quack. Quack. Quack.

The dogs waddled around the room, quacking like ducks.

"Oh no!" I wailed.

"This is horrible!" Liv groaned.

The bag! It messed up—again! It made duck-dogs!

The cats snarled and spat at the quacking terriers.

My room seethed with animals. Hissing cats wove between my feet. Quacking dogs surged around my ankles. There were so many of them, I couldn't even see my rug anymore.

I started to feel dizzy. So many animals in such a small space!

Then . . . the cats leaped at the dogs. With claws

bared, they tore after them. Quacking and yelping, the dogs ran for cover.

The room echoed with hissing, screeching, and quacking.

"It didn't work! Your stupid idea didn't work!" I yelled at Liv. "The dogs were supposed to chase the cats! But instead the cats are chasing the dogs!"

"It's not my fault. It's the bag's fault!" Liv snapped.

We watched as the cats pounced on the dogs.

Quack! Quack! Quack! The dogs tried frantically to escape. But I guess they weren't cut out for waddling.

Some just toppled over. Others tried to hide in my closet. Still others tried to squeeze under the bed.

One dog scrambled up on my drum set. He lost his balance and sent my drums and cymbals toppling over. They landed on the floor with a deafening *crash!*

"Greg!" Mom called up the stairs.

Uh-oh.

Now I was in real trouble.

I picked my way back to the door and opened it a crack. "What, Mom?" I called, trying to sound innocent.

"What is all that noise?" she demanded.

"Greg! Look out!" Liv shouted.

The dogs had followed me to the door.

They waddled out of the room.

49

The cats ran after them, chasing them down the steps.

My legs were all tangled up in cats and dogs. I couldn't stop them. I couldn't stop *myself*. It was all I could do to keep my balance as they dragged me downstairs with them. "Watch out, Mom!" I yelled.

My mother leaped back as I lunged for the front door. I opened it—and the cats chased the dogs right out of the house.

"Greg! *What* are you doing?" Mom gaped at the fleeing animals in shock.

I gulped. "Uh . . . Just cleaning my room."

Liv and I dashed out of the house before Mom or Dad could say another word. We ran past Mrs. O'Connor's house.

"Muffin . . . Where are you?" I heard her calling. "Muffin! Time to eat!"

We kept running.

We didn't stop until we reached the park on the other side of town.

Out of breath, we collapsed on the grass under a tree.

I closed my eyes—and pictured my room filled with hissing cats and quacking dogs.

"That was really scary!" I admitted to Liv.

I leaned back against the tree and sighed. Then I bolted upright as I thought of something terrible.

"Oh no!" I cried. "Princess! The real Princess! She must have run out with all the other cats. I wonder where she is?"

"Don't worry. I'm sure she'll find her way back home," Liv said. "But we *do* have to worry about that stupid trick-or-treat bag! We have to get rid of it, Greg. It's way too dangerous to have hanging around."

"I know. But I'm glad I had it," I said. I relaxed against the tree again. "It helped me beat Derek."

"The competition isn't over, Dreamer," Derek's voice said.

I jumped to my feet as he stepped out from behind the tree.

"How long were you there?" I demanded. "Were you spying on us?"

"Spying on you? Oh, please." Derek shook his head. "I've got better things to do, Dreamer."

"Like what?" I sneered.

A smug smile crept across Derek's face. "Like hanging out in my uncle's brand-new candy store." His smile grew broader. "Now I have so much more candy than you, it isn't even funny!"

I could feel my face begin to turn red.

How is this possible? I asked myself.

How can Derek have such good luck? How?

"And guess what else?" he went on. "Look what my grandmother gave me."

He shoved a thick stack of money in my face. "Five hundred dollars for my birthday today! Now I have more money than you, too," he bragged.

Derek's birthday is today? I thought miserably. How can I have such *bad* luck!

"I beat you!" Derek crowed. "I beat you after all!"

"No you didn't!" I blurted out. "I can have one thousand dollars by tomorrow!"

"Greg!" Liv warned.

I ignored her. "Just come to my house—and you'll see," I told Derek.

"Yeah, right." Derek smirked.

"Afraid you'll lose the bet?" I taunted.

"Ha. No chance. I'll see you tomorrow, loser." Derek walked off, laughing.

"Yeah. You're the loser, loser," I muttered to his back.

I strode out of the park. I was going home—home for the trick-or-treat bag.

"Greg, wait!" Liv ran after me. "I know what you're up to. You can't use that bag again! It's too dangerous!"

"I have to use it!" I told her. "Just one more time. I have to beat Derek!"

"But the money it makes is no good! It's counterfeit!"

"It looked real enough to fool us," I reminded her. "It will fool Derek, too. That's all I need."

I ran the rest of the way home. I couldn't wait to start making money—way more money than Derek. Liv ran next to me, trying to talk me out of it. But she was wasting her breath.

I ran up to my room.

The bag wasn't on the floor where I had left it.

In fact, I didn't see it anywhere.

"Where is it?" I muttered.

My heart began to pound. My eyes darted frantically around the room. Where was that bag? I needed it to beat Derek!

"Calm down. It has to be here somewhere," Liv assured me.

"It has to be—because I need it!" I cried. "I need a thousand dollars by tomorrow!"

I spun in a circle, searching everywhere.

But the bag was gone.

"Where is it?" I cried. "Where is my trick-or-treat bag?"

My books were back on the shelves. My homework sat neatly on my desk. The bed was made.

But there was no sign of the bag.

I threw my shoes out from under the bed, searching for it.

I flung the clothes out of my drawers.

I scattered the papers on my desk.

I couldn't find it anywhere.

"Stop looking!" Liv pleaded. "Forget about the bag!"

"But I need it!" I insisted. "If only I can find it, I can beat Derek once and for all."

I tore open the closet door. Started pulling clothes off the hangers. "Where is it? Where is it?"

"*Greg!*" Mom yelled. "*What* are you doing in here?"

I glanced up. She stood in the doorway with her arms crossed over her chest. "I just cleaned up your room. Now look at what you've done!"

"But Mom—"

"And you left it a mess after I told you to clean it up! Bringing all those animals in here. I tell you, Greg, I'm starting to lose patience with you."

"But Mom, I—"

"And my reading group is going to be here any minute. So clean this place—right now!" Mom turned to leave.

"Mom, *wait!*" I yelled.

She stopped in the doorway and raised her eyebrows at me.

I took a deep breath. "Did you see a big trick-or-treat bag with orange handles and a jack-o'-lantern on the front?"

"Yes. I did."

"Great! What did you do with it?"

"I tossed all your trash into it," she said.

Liv and I glanced nervously at each other.

"You put stuff *in* the bag?" I asked.

"Yes. That's what I said—I tossed all your trash into it. Then I threw the bag out."

I let out a gasp. "You threw the bag out?"

The doorbell rang.

"That must be my reading group." Mom hurried down the stairs to greet them.

"Oh no, Liv! She threw the bag out!" I bolted across the room to check my wastepaper basket.

Empty.

Liv and I tore through the second floor. We searched all the wastepaper baskets.

All empty.

"Face it, Greg," Liv said. "That bag is history."

"No, it's not." I snapped my fingers. "I know! Today is garbage day. It's probably in the garbage can out front!"

Liv and I raced downstairs. Mom's reading group was getting settled in the living room, so we had to run to the back door.

We dashed around to the front of the house.

Our big green garbage can sat by the curb.

I lifted the lid—and let out a long moan.

The garbage can was empty! The garbage truck had already come!

"Now what am I going to do?" I sat down on the curb with my head in my hands. "I need that bag."

"I still say you're better off without it," Liv declared. "I'm glad it's gone."

Gone.

My magic trick-or-treat bag was gone. Taken away by the trash collectors.

I bet Derek that I would have a thousand dollars. I bet him that I'd have it by tomorrow—and he was coming to see it.

I pictured his face when I showed him nothing.

He's never going to let me live this down, I realized.

"I can't lose this bet with Derek," I moaned. "I just can't."

Liv shrugged her shoulders.

"How much money do you have?" I asked her.

"None."

I checked my jeans pockets.

Empty.

I'm a loser, I thought. A big loser. What am I going to do now? Should I just leave town?

And then I heard it. The rumble of the garbage truck. It was grinding around the corner, heading back to the dump.

With my trick-or-treat bag in it. Somewhere.

"Come on, Liv!" I jumped up from the curb. "We have to catch that truck!"

12

~~~

I raced after the garbage truck.

The traffic light turned red on the corner of the next block. The garbage truck rumbled to a stop.

Yes! I thought.

I can catch it now!

I picked up speed.

I ran so hard I thought my lungs would burst.

The truck stood half a block away. The light remained red.

"Wait! I need my garbage back!" I shouted to the man behind the wheel.

The light turned green.

The truck didn't move.

He heard me!

I ran faster. My sneakers pounded the ground. I was almost there. I could almost touch the truck.

And then it pulled away.

"Oh no," I groaned. "He didn't hear me."

I started to run again. But the driver stepped hard on the gas. In seconds, the truck was disappearing down the road, blocks and blocks away, a tiny speck now.

Out of breath and disappointed, I trudged back to my house. Liv was still standing out front. She hadn't moved.

"Sorry. But it's the best thing that could have happened," she said as I walked up. "That bag was too weird."

I guess she was trying to make me feel better.

But she made me feel worse.

"Of course the bag was weird—it was a *magic* bag!" I shouted. "And you can't just give up a magic bag! We have to get it back. We have to go to the dump and find it."

"Are you nuts?" Liv yelled. "There's tons of garbage at the dump. We'll never find the stupid bag."

"If we hurry we will," I insisted. "It will be easy."

"We are not going to find that bag," Liv argued.

"Why not?"

"Because *we* are not going." Liv started to walk away. *"You* are going—without me. Good luck."

Good luck—I knew I couldn't count on that.

I needed Liv's help.

"Wait!" I called after her. "What if I promise to use the bag just one more time. Just once—so I can make the thousand dollars to beat Derek. Then I promise I'll get rid of it. Will you help me find it?"

Liv sat down on the curb, thinking. She twisted her braid around her finger.

I didn't want to rush her.

But we needed to get to the dump fast, before the bag was completely buried in trash.

I couldn't wait any longer. "Come on, Liv," I urged. "We have to hurry. Or we'll lose it forever!"

"Okay, okay," she finally agreed.

The dump was way out at the western edge of Shadyside. We ran the whole way there.

I'd never actually visited the place. But I knew it was on Oak Street. And I could tell from the smell when we got close.

Phew! What a stink.

We followed our noses, turned a corner—and there it was. Behind a tall wire fence—mountains and mountains of garbage. Some were piled way higher than my house.

"I'm not going in there! Look!" Liv shrieked. "Vultures!"

Clouds of dark birds circled the heaps. They dove down. Then snapped up bits of rancid food from the stinking mounds.

"Liv. They're not vultures. They're pigeons," I told her as I pulled her through a hole in the fence.

We walked around the tall piles of trash.

They smelled worse than rotten eggs. Worse than sour milk. Worse than skunk. Worse than all those three put together.

I almost gagged on the horrible stench. But I held my nose and pressed on. I had to find that bag!

"Ewwww!" Liv shrieked. "Get this off of me! Get it off now!" She jumped up and down like a maniac.

I turned to see her cheek smeared with brown glop.

I didn't know what the gooey stuff was, but it smelled really awful—and there were flies stuck in it.

I didn't want to make a big deal of it, so I wiped it off with my jacket sleeve. Yuck.

Then we continued to search.

I sifted through some small piles of trash.

I poked at some rotting cardboard boxes.

Nothing.

I turned in a circle and gazed at the mounds and mounds of garbage. It would take forever to search through it all.

"Hey! What's that?" Liv pointed to a small hill of trash a few feet ahead of us.

From the top, two orange handles peeked up—just like the handles on my trick-or-treat bag.

Yes!

I sprinted over to the hill for a closer look.

Definitely yes!

"You're a genius! You found it!" I cheered Liv.

I started to climb up the garbage hill. My foot sank in—up to my ankle. I could feel my sneaker and sock turn wet. Wet and slimy.

I didn't stop to think about it—or to look. I had to keep going.

I climbed and climbed until I reached the bag.

"I've got it!" I grabbed the bag, waved it in the air for Liv to see—and lost my balance.

I toppled down the other side of the garbage hill.

I rolled head over heels all the way to the bottom. I landed in a deep pit of blackish brown slime.

"Greg! Are you okay?" Liv ran around the mountain of garbage to help. "Ewww! That's disgusting." She backed away from me fast.

I was covered in the oily ooze. My clothes. My face. My hair. Drops of it clung to my eyelashes.

I tried to stand up.

My sneakers slid on the oily muck. My feet flew out from under me. I landed on my back with a sickening plop—drenched in the sludge.

"I can't get up. You'll have to help me." I reached out my hand for Liv to grab.

"You're filthy and you stink! I'm not touching you."

"Liv!"

"Okay, okay." She took my filthy hand. "Oh,

gross." Gagging and coughing, she pulled me out of the pit.

On the way back to my house, Liv walked on the other side of the street. As far away from me as she could. She couldn't stand the way I smelled.

I guess I really reeked.

We sneaked in through the back door so that Mom and her reading group wouldn't see me. I prayed they wouldn't smell me either.

I dropped the bag on my bedroom floor. Then I headed into the bathroom to wash up and change my clothes.

"Greg! Come quick! Come back here!" Liv cried.

I ran out of the bathroom—and stopped in my doorway.

Liv was standing on my bed.

"Th-the bag," she stammered, pointing to the floor. "There's something in it!"

13

The bag bulged. It twisted and curled on the floor. Then it uncurled and thrashed.

I watched in horror as it seemed to inflate—growing fuller and fuller.

"Wh-what do you think is in there?" Liv twisted her braid around her entire hand.

"I don't know." My voice was hushed and fearful. "But whatever it is, it's multiplying."

I couldn't imagine *what* was in there. The bag felt empty when I carried it home.

I watched its seams strain to keep closed.

What was in there?

Liv gasped as the bag started to pitch and reel across my room. It seemed alive now.

"Did you see my hamster?" Raina popped her head into my room. "I let him out of his cage this morning. I've looked everywhere. I can't find him."

"Oh no," I groaned. "Liv, did the hamster run in here while I was in the bathroom?"

"I—I didn't see him. But I guess he could have," she replied.

"Why are you standing on the bed?" Raina asked Liv. "Mom doesn't allow that."

"It's your fault!" I told my sister as I reached for the bag. "If you hadn't let your hamster out—"

I carefully lifted up one of the handles of the bag. I peeked inside—and cried out in shock.

"Cockroaches!"

Thousands of cockroaches swarmed out of the bag. They surged into my room.

They moved across the floor in waves. A brown sea of disgusting cockroaches.

With wriggling antennae, they probed the air— then scattered!

They scampered up the curtains and along my furniture. They swarmed over my desk.

Streams of them continued to pour out of the bag. They must have made a nest in there—and then multiplied!

Within seconds, the floor, the walls, and the ceiling were alive with scurrying roaches.

Raina opened her mouth to scream, but no sound came out. She ran from the room.

The roaches crawled up my bed, along my blanket—and up Liv's legs.

"Get them off me!" She jumped up and down on the mattress, shrieking.

Roaches crawled up my pants. They crawled up my arms. I swiped them away. Swiped madly.

But they kept coming.

And then they started to bite.

I suddenly felt hundreds of tiny nips all over my body. "Ow!" I yelled. "Ow! Ouch!"

"Yeow!" Liv screamed, slapping at her arms and legs. "They're eating me!"

"Roaches aren't supposed to bite!" I yelled.

"It's the bag's fault!" Liv screamed. "The copies it makes are evil, Greg!"

I felt a roach creep across my cheek.

I swatted it from my face.

Another one dropped from the ceiling—and landed in my hair.

"Oooooo!" I brushed my hand through my hair quickly. I hung my head down and shook it hard.

I spun around to the mirror to see if it was gone—but I couldn't see a thing.

The mirror was covered with a thick, brown blanket—a living blanket of roaches.

They crawled in and out of my VCR, my radio, my TV.

"What are we going to do?" Liv wailed. She batted roaches from her neck. "This is all your fault! I told you to leave that bag where it was! I told you it was dangerous!"

Her hand flew up to her face. "Oh, *gross!*" She flicked one out of her ear. "Do something!" she screamed.

I crossed the room to get my baseball mitt. I'll try to scoop them up, I thought.

I took a few steps—and let out a moan.

A carpet of roaches crunched under my feet.

I sucked in a deep breath and lunged across the room for my glove.

Then I started to scoop.

That's when the roaches started to fly.

14

The roaches didn't just *fly*.

They *dive-bombed* us.

They swooped down from the ceiling and zoomed at our faces. The room hummed with the sound of their wings.

"Greg, this is a nightmare!" Liv cried out. "They're attacking us! Roaches are *not* supposed to do that!"

A squadron of roaches soared at me. I batted them back. I swiped furiously at them.

They circled me.

They landed on my head. I could feel their legs—hundreds of roach legs—crawling over my scalp.

I scratched and scratched—and they flew into my

ears. They scuttled across my face. Their sharp legs pricked my eyelids.

I shook my head wildly, trying to get them off.

A brown cloud of the insects dove for Liv.

"Watch out!" I screamed—and a roach flew into my mouth.

It lodged in my throat.

My stomach heaved.

I started to gag.

I opened my mouth and forced myself to cough. I bent over and coughed hard. Finally the bug flew out of my mouth.

"Ooooo, gross. *Gross!*" I collapsed on the floor. *CRUNCH! CRUNCH!*

Yuck!

Liv leaped off the bed. "We can't catch this many roaches. We have to get out of here. They're out of control!"

She raced into the hallway.

I got up and ran out after her—and gasped.

The hall was a moving brown river of roaches. Roaches marching toward Raina's bedroom—and Mom and Dad's too.

"We have to stop them!" I ran to the linen closet and pulled out a stack of towels.

"Quick!" I told Liv. "Close the bedroom doors and block the bottoms with these." I tossed a thick stack of towels to her.

I ran to Raina's room. It was right next to mine.

Raina sat under her blankets. "I found him," she said meekly, cuddling her hamster. They both shivered with fear.

"Just stay there," I told her. "You'll be okay." I slammed her door shut and blocked the cracks with towels.

"No roaches here," Liv called from Mom and Dad's room down the hall.

She closed the door and sealed off the bottom with some towels.

I headed across the hall to the bathroom.

Too late.

Roaches skittered across the white tile floor. They swarmed in the tub. They crept over the toilet seat.

I peered into the toilet bowl—and saw at least fifty of them paddling around.

Ugh.

I raced for the steps—and froze.

Thousands of roaches swarmed down the stairs.

They crawled along the banister.

They scuttled along the walls.

They soared through the air.

The ones crawling down the steps were the worst. I watched in horror as the big ones scurried right over the backs of the little ones in a race to get down.

"Roaches! Roaches!" Shrieks and cries rose suddenly from the living room.

Oh, no!

Mom's reading group!

I bolted down the steps, two at a time, trying to ignore the crunching under my feet.

I peeked into the living room.

Everyone was hopping desperately around the room. Leaping and jumping over the roaches. One lady was standing in the middle of the coffee table, screaming.

I winced as a huge roach fluttered into her mouth. I should have warned her about opening her mouth.

Everyone swatted at the bugs. Batted them. Stomped on them.

"This is disgusting!" a tall, thin woman cried. "I'm leaving."

She picked up her book—and let out a scream. A small army of roaches crawled out from between the pages. They marched up her fingers.

"Ouch! They bite!" she wailed.

I watched as all the color drained from Mom's face.

She chased after the roaches with a dish towel. "I'm so sorry," she apologized in a frantic voice. "I don't know where they came from. I really don't. I've never had this problem before."

Mom swung the dish towel around the room.

Smacking, beating, slapping, whacking at the horrible bugs.

It wasn't working.

They scattered to other parts of the room.

I glanced up the steps.

More roaches headed down.

A lot more.

"Greg! Help!" Mom spotted me, her eyes wide with panic. "Get the bug spray. *Hurry!*"

I raced into the kitchen. I searched under the sink for the spray.

We didn't have any.

It wouldn't have worked anyway. Mom didn't know it, but we had thousands and thousands of roaches. We'd need a tank of that stuff to get rid of them.

"What are you going to do?" Liv met me in the kitchen. She kept scratching at her skin. "How are you going to get rid of them?"

"We can't do this alone," I said.

I tore back upstairs.

Crunch. Crunch. Crunch.

Cockroaches crunched under my pounding feet.

I grabbed the trick-or-treat bag.

I shook it to make sure it was empty. Then I raced back downstairs. I grabbed Liv and we ran out of the house.

We charged through the neighborhood.

"Where are we going?" Liv panted.

"Don't worry! Just follow me!"

"Follow you *where?*" she asked, gulping for air.

"We need help!" I cried. "We're going for help!"

"Where?" Liv demanded.

"We have to see that old lady!" I cried. "She's the only one who can help us. We're going to Fear Street!"

15

"**F**ear Street!" Liv stopped running. "I'm not going back there. No way!"

"We have no choice, Liv. My house is crawling with cockroaches. Flying, stinging, biting cockroaches! We have to talk to that old woman. It's her bag. She knows how it works. She'll know how to get rid of them!"

I started walking.

Liv didn't move.

She planted her feet firmly on the ground. Her face turned rigid.

"You'll have to find another way to get rid of the roaches," she declared. "I'm not going with you."

"You have to go with me!" I shouted.

"Why? Why do I have to go with you? All this was your fault—not mine!" Liv yelled. "I told you not to chase after that bag. But you wouldn't listen!"

"I thought you were my best friend! But you're not! You're not even a *good* friend!" I shouted.

I didn't mean to say that to Liv. She *was* a good friend. I was just upset.

She won't take it seriously, I told myself.

She'll laugh it off—then she'll go with me.

I waited.

Liv wasn't laughing.

"Not a good friend!" she exploded. "Since this morning, I've been scratched by killer cats. I've been attacked by quacking dogs. I was nearly sent to jail. I've had garbage flies stuck to my face and cockroaches crawling in my ears. All because of *you!* I'm going home!"

"You can't go," I argued.

"Try to stop me!" Liv started to walk away.

"Please, Liv!" I chased after her. "I'm sorry about what I said. It's just that I have a big problem right now. I have to get rid of the roaches! Please, please come with me."

"No! I am not going into that creepy woman's house again!" Liv quickened her step.

"We won't go in!" I panted, trying to catch up with her. "We'll ring the bell. When the old woman comes to the door, I'll ask her what to do. We'll stay on the porch. We won't go in—I promise."

Liv stopped walking.

She twisted her braid, thinking. "You really, really promise?"

I nodded.

"Okay."

"Thanks. You *are* a great friend. Now let's go!"

We raced to the old woman's house.

Fear Street was as spooky as ever. The late afternoon sun had faded, and the streetlights should have been on. But they weren't.

As we neared the end of the block, an icy wind began to blow. The tree limbs quaked and groaned in the strong gusts.

"This is it." I touched Liv's arm to stop her.

We stood directly in front of the old woman's house.

I stared at it. The grimy bricks. The totally dark windows.

"Remember—you promised we wouldn't go in." Liv's voice trembled.

I nodded.

We walked up the path to the front door.

I knocked softly at first.

No answer.

"I think this is a big mistake." Liv twisted her

braid around her fingers. "Don't knock again. We'll figure out how to get rid of the roaches ourselves. I really think we should go home."

I knocked again. A little harder this time.

The door creaked open.

Ricky, the kid we had met the first time we were there, answered. He stood in the dim light of the entranceway. Behind him I could see the glow of the candles. I could hear the clocks. Ticking. Ticking. Ticking.

"Hi, Ricky," I said. "I need to ask your, um, mother a question."

Ricky stared at us. His skin appeared even paler than before. The blue veins in his face seemed brighter.

I waited for him to say something—but he didn't.

"Um, Greg means your grandmother," Liv tried. "We have to ask your grandmother a question."

Silence.

"It will just take a second," I said.

Ricky stepped forward.

His face twisted into a scowl.

"Get away!" he said gruffly. "Get away *now!*"

16

"**G**o!" Ricky commanded. His eyes bulged open.

Liv spun around and started to leave.

"Wait!" A strong hand grasped my wrist and pulled me inside the house. "I'm so glad to see you. I knew you'd come back."

It was the old woman.

She wore the same black velvet shirt. The same long skirt. The same jewelry. Everything the same— except now she had bright orange lipstick smeared across her lips.

Her orange lips parted in an icy smile.

I did *not* want to be inside this house alone.

"Liv! Come back!" I called out the door. I could see

her scurrying down the path. She was nearly at the gate.

"Please come back!"

Would she really leave me here—alone with this creepy old woman?

Liv stopped.

She turned around and stared at me. She twisted her braid.

"Please!"

I let out a sigh of relief when she started back and followed me inside.

We stood close together in the big living room. It looked as creepy as it had the first time we were there.

The pink and purple crystals glowed in the candle-light.

The owl stared down at us.

The clocks ticked. Ticked loudly.

The flickering candles made our shadows shift on the walls.

Ricky shrank back, behind the old woman. His hands seemed to tremble.

"I see you brought back the bag. I knew you would. I knew you'd come back to thank me." The old woman placed a hand on my shoulder.

A chill swept through my body.

I glanced at Liv.

She stood still. Frozen. Scared.

"I, um, have a question to ask you. See, I have these roaches in my house—" I started.

"Come in. Sit down." The old woman put her other hand on Liv's shoulder. Then she shoved us toward the crumbling couch.

"My mother will be here soon to pick us up," Liv lied. "We can't stay long—"

"Yes. I'm sure your mother will be here soon," the old lady said. I could tell she didn't believe Liv. "But we have plenty of time. Now sit!"

We sat.

The woman reached out and snatched the bag from me. "Thanks for returning this. I hope you enjoyed it. Now I think I'll show you some other tricks you can do with it."

"What do you mean?" I asked.

"Watch." The old woman turned and beckoned to Ricky. "Come here!" she said sharply.

Ricky stood across from us in an unlit corner of the room. Even in the dark, I could see him shaking.

We shouldn't have come here, I thought. *Liv was right.* We should have figured out a way to get rid of the roaches ourselves.

"It-it's okay," I said. "We can come back another time to see tricks. We . . . uh . . . we really have to be going now."

I stood up to leave.

"You're not going anywhere." The old lady's voice turned rough. Her face hardened. She pushed me back down on the couch.

Liv and I stared at each other.

"Not until I show you some magic," the old woman added. Her voice softened, but that made it even creepier.

"I know a lot of tricks," she told us, smiling. "And a lot of spells. I could put a spell on you right now . . . in a blink! And you wouldn't even know it happened!"

I glanced at the table beside the couch, at the book I had seen before—the one that said *"Magic"* in gold letters.

Liv leaned over. "She's crazy," she whispered. "We've got to get out of here."

The old woman glared at us. "Don't you know it's rude to whisper?" she snarled.

I gulped. "Maybe we'll stay for one trick," I said lamely.

"Ricky! Didn't I tell you to come here?" the old woman scolded.

Ricky moved out from the corner, slowly.

"Hurry up!" She narrowed her eyes at the frail boy. "These nice children want to see some magic!"

Ricky's legs trembled as he reached the old woman.

He stood in front of her, shaking all over now.

The old woman smiled. "Are you ready, Ricky?"

She didn't wait for his answer.

She lifted the trick-or-treat bag—and yanked it down over his head!

17

"No! Don't!" I screamed as the old lady lowered the bag over Ricky's shoulders.

"Run, Ricky!" Liv screamed.

But Ricky stood still. Frozen.

The old woman's lips moved. Low, growling sounds came out of her lips. Words in some weird, foreign language.

I gasped.

She was casting a spell!

An icy breeze sighed through the room. The candles flickered and sputtered.

Then the old lady whipped the bag off the boy— and he was gone.

"Where is he?" I stared at the empty space where Ricky had stood. "Where did Ricky go?"

The woman gazed into my eyes. Her pupils grew large and dark. I could see the candlelight flickering in them.

"Why, he's right here." She chuckled.

Then she glanced down.

I followed her gaze—and gasped.

There was Ricky, hunched on the floor.

But he wasn't Ricky anymore.

He was a frog.

"Ribbit," he croaked. *"Ribbit. Ribbit."*

"You turned him into a *frog!"* Liv cried out in shock.

The old woman smiled. "I told you I know all sorts of tricks. Wasn't that a good one?"

She knelt down. She tickled the frog's head. "He's a cute frog, isn't he?"

We stood in shocked silence.

She narrowed her eyes at us. "Don't you think he's a cute frog?" she asked sharply.

I nodded. I didn't know what else to do.

"I knew you'd agree. He's a very cute frog." She tickled the frog's belly. "I hope he enjoyed being a boy for a few days."

"You mean—he was *never* a real boy?" I asked in disbelief.

"No. He was just a frog. A frog I turned into a boy for a little while."

The old lady gave the frog a final pat on the head. Then she straightened up and began pacing the room. "Now, let's see. Let's see."

She stopped pacing. She stared at us. Studied us. "Let's see . . . What shall I do with you two?"

I grabbed Liv's arm. I jumped up from the couch. "Let's *go!*"

We ran for the door.

We were halfway there when the old woman let out a soft giggle.

I turned to glance at her. She lifted her right hand high.

She drew three circles in the air and began to chant:

> *"Creature of prey.*
> *Creature of night.*
> *Watchful creature.*
> *Creature take flight!"*

"Hoooo!" The cry of an owl echoed through the room.

We heard the soft flutter of wings—and then we saw it.

The owl on top of the grandfather clock was alive! It shook out its wing feathers.

85

Then it took to the air.

It soared down at us.

Circled us.

It let out another sharp cry. Then it swooped toward my face with outstretched talons.

I threw my hands over my head. I tried to dodge it. But it kept coming at me. First from the left. Then from the right.

"Stop it! Stop it!" Liv cried out.

The owl dove for her. Grazed the top of her head.

It circled us, cutting off our escape. Forcing us back into the room.

"I see you've changed your minds." The old woman's lips parted into a satisfied smile. "You've decided to stay after all."

She raised her left hand—and the owl returned to its perch. Its wings fluttered one last time. Then the life flickered out of its eyes.

"Now . . . where was I?" The old woman rested her chin in the palm of her hand and gazed at us.

"Let us go!" I shouted.

"I'm sorry, but I can't do that," she replied.

"Why not?" Liv wailed. "We brought the bag back. What else do you want?"

"What else do I want?" the old woman asked. "Why, I want some new pets—of course. Now . . . what shall I turn you into?"

18

"**H**mm. Would you like to be a llama?" The old woman gave me a wicked smile.

"A llama!" I cried out.

"Not a llama? No. Maybe you're right." She shook her head. "A llama would be too big for a house pet."

She thought for a moment. "How about goats?" Her eyes brightened. "You'd make a sweet pair of goats."

"I don't want to be a goat!" Liv cried. "I want to go home!"

The old woman's gaze turned icy. She stepped up to Liv. "Squeal, squeal. I think I'll make *you* a pig! Doesn't she sound like a pig?" she asked me.

I didn't answer. I couldn't.

"Now, let me see. Pigs require a special spell. I hope I can remember it." She closed her eyes to think.

"Greg, I don't want to be a pig!" Liv cried. "Do something!"

"Ribbit. Ribbit." Ricky leaped across the room and landed on the woman's foot. *"Ribbit. Ribbit."* He stared up at her with his big, bulging frog eyes and croaked.

"Of course. That's it!" The old lady's eyelids flew open. "I'll turn you both into frogs. I do love frogs."

She glanced down at Ricky. Her gaze softened. "And Ricky would like some new friends."

Frogs?

Forget it!

I grabbed Liv's hand and ran to a narrow archway that led to the next room. Maybe we'll find a back door there, I hoped.

In three short strides, we reached the arch. But as soon as we did, a door swung closed from the other side. It slammed in our faces.

The old woman shrieked with delight. "I told you— I know all sorts of tricks! Now come here before I lose my patience!"

Liv and I shrank back against the door.

"If you don't cooperate, I'll make your frog skin bubble with boils," the old lady warned.

We didn't move.

"Fine. Have it your way." The old woman approached us slowly, swinging the trick-or-treat bag in her hand.

"Okay. Which one of you wants to go first?" she asked as she stepped up to us.

We didn't answer.

"Is somebody going to speak?" She shifted her gaze from Liv to me.

We remained silent.

"Fine. I'll choose." She lifted the bag—and started to lower it over my head.

"Better say good-bye to your friend now," she told me. "Because in a few seconds, you'll only be able to croak."

19

"**N**oooo!" I screamed.

I grabbed the old woman's shoulders. I tried to shove her away.

But she was too strong. She didn't lose her balance. Not even a tiny bit.

"Be still!" she commanded sternly.

And suddenly, I couldn't move! It was as if my arms were strapped to my sides. My legs rooted to the floor.

The old woman lowered the bag slowly over my head. And there was nothing I could do to stop her.

The fabric slid over my hair.

Over my forehead.

As she pushed the bag down, the old lady chanted a spell in a low voice.

My face grew warm. My skin began to tingle.

"Leave him alone!" Liv shouted. She kicked the woman hard in the shin.

"Owwww!" The old lady let out a startled cry and bent down to rub her leg.

The kick must have broken her concentration or something. Because suddenly I could move again. My hands shot up. I ripped the bag off my head.

"You can't escape me!" she snarled.

She started to straighten up—and I quickly slipped the bag over her head!

I yanked it down. Over her face. Over her chin. Down to her shoulders.

The old woman twisted inside the bag, struggling to break free.

"Hold her arms, Liv," I yelled as the old woman thrashed inside the bag. "Don't let her out!"

"You can't do this to me!" the woman shrieked.

She struggled harder.

She twisted her body fiercely, left and right. She squirmed and kicked.

She tried to grab for me, but Liv held her arms in place.

And then I lifted the bag from her head.

I let her out.

And, in what seemed like the blink of an eye, *two* identical old women stood before me.

20

"Oh no!" Liv gasped. "There are two of them! How could you do this, Greg? How?"

"He didn't do anything." One of the old women leered. *"I* did it! Now there are two of us! Two of us—to get the two of you!"

The old women glared at us.

Their orange lips parted slowly.

"Now!" they both cried out—and lunged for us.

Liv and I bolted—but those old ladies were fast.

One chased Liv around the couch. The other reached out and grabbed for my arm. She caught my sleeve and tugged me toward her, hard.

"Give me that bag!" she screeched, groping for the trick-or-treat bag, which I held in my other hand.

"No!" I swung it behind my back, out of her reach.

The other woman caught Liv. She held her tightly. "*I* want that trick-or-treat bag!" she said. She glared at the woman who held me. "*You* wouldn't know what to do with it!" she screamed at her.

Then she shifted her gaze toward me. "Give it to me, boy," she said sweetly. "Give me the bag—and I'll let you go."

"Don't believe her!" Liv cried. "Don't give it to her! Don't let either of them have it!"

Would she really let us go? I wondered.

What should I do?

My head throbbed as the two women stared at me. Waiting. Waiting to see if I would give up the bag.

What should I do? What should I do? I asked myself.

Everyone's gaze remained on the bag.

What should I do? I asked myself again.

And, suddenly, I knew exactly what to do.

I held out the bag to the woman who held Liv.

"Are you *crazy?*" Liv screamed.

The old woman let Liv go and lunged for the bag.

"Noooo!" the woman who held me cried.

She pounced for the bag too—and let me go.

My plan worked! We were free!

I leaped back, out of reach of both women. They grabbed for me—but I wasn't there anymore. They crashed into each other and fell to the floor.

And I still held the trick-or-treat bag in my hand!

"Run!" I shouted to Liv.

We made it to the front door.

"Stop them!" I heard one of the women cry. "They're getting away with the bag!"

I tried to turn the doorknob.

It didn't move!

"Hurry!" Liv screamed. "They're coming!"

I tried to yank the door open.

It didn't budge.

"There must be another door!" Liv shouted. "We have to find it!"

We turned—and froze.

The two horrible old women stood before us, blocking our way.

Before I knew what was happening, one of them had reached out and snatched the bag from my grasp.

She turned to her twin. "Time for you to go!" she cackled.

She lifted the bag. She started to bring it down over the other old lady's head.

The other old lady grabbed my arm.

She shoved me in front of her.

And the bag came down—over *my* head!

21

"**W**hoops!" The old woman who held the bag giggled. She lifted it off my head.

I squeezed my eyes shut. I couldn't bear to look. "Am I okay?" I tried to ask Liv.

But all that came out was a long, loud *"Cluuuuck!"*

"Liv! What happened!" I tried to yell.

"Cluck! Cluck! Cluck!" came out of my mouth.

"Oh no! You turned him into a chicken!" Liv shrieked in horror.

My eyes popped open. I bent my head and stared at my body.

Feathers.

I was covered in reddish brown feathers.

"Cluck! Cluck! Cluuuuuck!" My beak quivered.

I glared up at the old woman who had done this to me. My head bobbed up and down as I pecked at her foot. I pecked hard!

"Turn me back!" I screamed at her.

But all that came out was, *"Cluck! Cluuuuck!"*

"What a nice chicken." She bent down and stroked my head. "I do love fresh eggs for breakfast!"

She ruffled my feathers—and Liv grabbed the bag from her!

She bolted across the room.

"Give that back to me!" the old woman shrieked.

"No! Give it to *me! Me!*" her twin yelled. "Give it to *me*—and I'll turn your friend back into a boy!"

"Don't make promises you can't keep. I'm the one with the magic, not you!" The old woman shoved her twin hard. "You have no magic. *I'm* the one with the power. *I'm* the one who knows the spells. I *made* you!"

I fluttered across the room to Liv. She scooped me up. She smoothed down my feathers and tucked me under her arm.

The old women were screaming at each other. One lunged for the other's throat. They wrestled each other to the floor.

"We're going to try to sneak out," Liv whispered to me. "I'm going to try to find another door."

She moved across the room slowly. Step by step. Trying not to attract any attention.

It wasn't hard. The old women didn't notice us. They were too busy tearing at each other's clothes. Pulling each other's hair.

Liv kept inching across the room. Slowly. Slowly.

I stared at the struggling old ladies.

One of the old women suddenly tore herself free and jumped up. "I'm going to finish you off," she panted, aiming a bony finger at her twin. She grabbed a pink crystal from a nearby table.

She held it in front of a candle's flame.

She stared into its warm, pink glow.

"Noooo!" the other woman shrieked. She leaped to her feet. Her eyes darted frantically around the room—searching, searching for something.

Then she found it—the book called *Magic.*

She picked it up and flipped madly through its pages.

At last she must have found the right page. She ran her finger down it, reading swiftly. Mumbling the words. Repeating them over and over. Memorizing them.

Liv took another step—and another. No one paid any attention to us.

The first old woman continued to stare deep into the crystal. She held it before the flame. She stared at it, in a trance. Then she began to chant:

"Glowing crystal, glowing bright,
Gathering strength in candlelight.
This old woman we will banish;
With your power, make her vanish—"

"Stop!" the other woman shrieked. She made a grab for the crystal.

Now they both held on to it tightly—and they both screamed out the last part of the chant:

"The one who holds the crystal near
Will make the other disappear!"

There was a moment of absolute silence. No one moved. No one breathed.

Even the clocks stopped ticking.

And then . . .

Both old ladies started to fade.

Liv froze in midstep.

We watched in amazement as their figures grew more and more transparent.

They faded and faded. In a few seconds we could see right through them.

And then they disappeared.

A loud *cluck* escaped from my throat—and my head started to hurt. It was stuck under Liv's armpit!

My head!

My real head!

The old ladies were gone—the spell was broken.

I was a kid again!

"Ow!" I cried. My voice was muffled against Liv's shirt. "Let go of me!"

Liv shrieked and threw her arms up. I stumbled free of her grasp.

"You're back!" Liv cheered. "Hooray!"

We charged for the front door and raced out of the house.

We ran all the way down Fear Street. Under the gnarled tree branches that blocked out the moonlight. Past the gloomy front yards. Past the crumbling houses.

We didn't stop running until we reached my house.

"I can't believe that happened," Liv panted. "I just can't believe it. I'm never going to Fear Street again. Never."

"*You* can't believe it!" I cried. "I turned into a chicken!"

For the first time all day, Liv laughed.

But her grin quickly faded when she saw what I held in my hand. Her green eyes flickered with fear.

"How did you get *that?*" She pointed at the trick-or-treat bag I held.

"I grabbed it off the floor when we ran out of the house. But don't worry about it," I told her.

"Don't worry about it!" Liv put her hands on her hips. "What do you mean, don't worry about it? You can't use it again! That bag is trouble! You have to get rid of it!"

"I know," I said. "That's why I took it. I'm going to bury it somewhere—a safe place where no one can find it."

"Promise?" Liv begged.

"I promise. I'm not going to use it. I've learned my lesson. It's much too dangerous. Really. I've learned my lesson. . . ."

22

Liv burst through our kitchen door. "Muffin is back!" she announced.

"Where?" My eyes darted around the kitchen, looking for him.

"Relax." Liv laughed. "He's in Mrs. O'Connor's front yard. I walked by him on my way over here. I guess he found his way home okay yesterday."

It was the next morning—the morning after our second visit to Fear Street. I guess I was still a little jumpy.

"Are you sure it was the real Muffin?" I asked, opening the cabinet under the sink.

"I'm sure." Liv took a seat at the table. "He wasn't

waddling, and he nearly bit my hand off when I tried to pet him."

Liv glanced at the table, where I had placed my sneakers. They were the sneakers I had worn to the garbage dump—and they were pretty filthy.

"Phew. You're not going to *wear* these, are you?" She held her nose. "They stink!"

"I know." I peered inside the cabinet. "I'm looking for something to use to clean them."

"I'm telling." I heard Raina's irritating voice from the doorway.

I pulled my head out of the cabinet. "You're telling *what?*"

"I'm telling Mom you put your sneakers on the table." She turned to Liv. "Mom says we're not supposed to put our shoes on the furniture."

"Hey, look who's here!" Liv glanced at the door. Princess sauntered in.

I watched Princess as she entered the kitchen.

Was she *our* Princess—or one of the copies?

I stretched out my hand to stroke her head.

"Don't touch her!" Raina screamed.

I jerked my hand back. "Why not?"

"Because she's *my* cat!" Raina scooped Princess up and left the room.

I let out a sigh.

Liv suddenly jumped up from her seat. She glanced nervously around the kitchen.

"What's wrong?" I asked.

"I just remembered. What happened to all the roaches?"

"They're gone. Mom called an exterminator to get rid of them," I explained. "But she's still pretty upset. I don't think her reading group is ever going to come back here."

"And what about the bag?" Liv continued to scan the room. "Did you hide the trick-or-treat bag?"

I nodded.

"Did you hide it where no one will find it?" she pressed.

"Uh-huh," I answered. "I buried it under some rocks in Shadyside Park." I paused. "But first—uh—first I used it one more time."

"What do you mean?" Liv's voice rose. "How could you! You promised!"

I didn't answer.

"What did you do with it?" She was shouting now.

"Calm down," I told her. "Come up to my room and I'll show you."

"I don't believe you," Liv mumbled, shaking her head, as we walked up the stairs. "After everything that happened—how could you use that bag!"

We walked down the hall to my bedroom. Liv squinted at me. "Why is the door closed?" she asked, twirling her braid around her fingers.

I didn't reply.

I just opened the door slowly.

Liv poked her head in the doorway—and shrieked!

23

"**H**i, Liv." One of the Gregs in my room waved to her. He sat on the floor, refolding my shirts.

When he was finished, another Greg organized them in my drawer by color.

A different Greg tucked the sheet under my mattress. Then he smoothed the blanket out on top—while another crawled under the bed with a feather duster.

My room was filled with Gregs. All together there were ten of me!

It was awesome to see!

"You made copies of yourself!" Liv stared at all the Gregs in disbelief. "What are they doing?"

"They're cleaning," I said. "They're like me—but not exactly. They're neat."

"We're finally going to beat Derek!" One of the Gregs cheered.

"Yes!" Another one pumped his fist in the air. "Ten Gregs and only one Derek!"

All the Gregs laughed.

"I've got to sit down." Liv walked over to my bed and plopped down. She looked sort of pale.

"This is the day, Liv!" I told her. "Today is my lucky day. Today is the day I win! There are ten of me—and only one of him! Derek will never beat that. Never!"

"From now on Greg will always be the winner!" another Greg declared.

"Oh, really?" Liv murmured. She was staring out my window. "Um—I wouldn't be so sure of that."

"Huh? What are you talking about?" I stepped up to the window.

I stared outside—and gasped.

There was Derek, marching up to my house.

In his hand he carried the magic trick-or-treat bag.

Next to him walked another Derek. And next to that Derek, another. And another. And another. . . .

I counted the Dereks—and screamed.

There were ten of me.

But there were *twenty* of him!

Are you ready for another walk
down Fear Street?
Turn the page for a terrifying
sneak preview.

GO TO YOUR TOMB—
RIGHT NOW!

Coming mid-October 1997

I took one last, long look at the stone face carved in the mausoleum door.

It wasn't warm. It wasn't alive. I must have imagined it.

"Okay," I said at last. "Let's go."

Connor and I went down the steps of the stone tomb and started to walk away.

I heard something creak behind me. I stopped.

It sounded like a door.

"Come on, Jack," Connor said impatiently.

Obviously, he didn't hear anything. I began walking again.

We were in the Fear Street Cemetery. The only door around here was the mausoleum door.

But there was no one in there to open it.

No one alive, anyway.

I picked up my pace.

"Wait! Stop, please!" called a voice.

This time we both heard it. A girl's voice.

Connor and I stopped and turned around slowly.

In front of the mausoleum stood a girl.

My mouth dropped open as I stared at her. She beckoned to us with a long, pale hand.

She seemed about our age, maybe a little older.

And she looked an awful lot like the stone face on the mausoleum door.

My mouth moved—but no words came out.

"It's her!" I finally whispered.

She glided toward us. The wind whipped her blond hair around her face.

Her eyes locked on to mine. They were the same color as her velvet dress—a deep, dark blue. She didn't speak. She just kept staring at me with those sad, blue eyes.

Who was she? Where did she come from?

Was she a ghost?

I took a step back. I wanted to run.

I wanted to run fast and never look back.

But my feet were frozen to the spot.

"What do you want?" Connor demanded.

She smiled. "My name is Luana. I come from a different time," she told us calmly. "And a different place."

She stared at me again. Tiny shivers ran up my spine.

But I couldn't say a word.

"Hundreds of years ago my family and I were servants of a powerful sorcerer. Powerful and evil," the girl continued. She paused and gazed off into space.

Connor nudged me with his elbow. "Yeah, sure. And I'm actually from the planet Pluto," he whispered to me.

Luana snapped back to attention. "Please don't joke with me. I'm quite serious," she said sternly.

"Oh, sorry." Connor got a patient look on his face, the one he got when he thought I was being dumb. "Tell us more."

Luana went on, "This evil sorcerer caught me in his precious library, reading his spell books. He was furious. The secrets of his magic were not for a servant like me."

She paused for breath. I glanced uncertainly at Connor.

He still had that patient look on his face.

He wasn't buying any of it.

"The sorcerer imprisoned me in this tomb," she

continued, pointing to the mausoleum. "I was to live out my days here—until someone freed me."

She held her hand out to me. "Thank you. *You* freed me! You saved me from an eternity in stone."

I didn't want to touch her. I didn't want to have anything to do with her. It was all too spooky.

But she kept holding out her hand to me. At last I grabbed it and gave it a quick squeeze.

It was warm. She was definitely real—not a ghost. I breathed a sigh of relief.

"Now I need your help once again," she said. "Please help me get back to my time and my family. Please."

Connor nudged me with his elbow. "Come on, Jack. Let's get out of here." He glared at Luana. "I bet the Burger brothers put you up to this stupid trick. Or maybe Penny."

"It is not a trick!" Luana cried. "And I don't know anyone named Penny. Or the Burger brothers. Please believe me."

"Let's go, Jack," Connor urged. He tugged on my arm.

I pulled away from him. "I don't know." I glanced at the face on the door. "That's her face carved there."

Connor grabbed my arm again. "It *isn't* her. It could be any girl. Let's go."

Luana stared at me with her sad eyes. I felt as though she could see right through me.

"This is dumb. I'm out of here," Connor grumbled. He started to walk away.

I hurried after him. "What if she's telling the truth?" I asked in a low voice. "She came out of the mausoleum."

Connor didn't stop walking. "Jack, you are hopeless. Did you see the tomb door open?"

"No," I admitted lamely. "But I heard a noise—"

"But you didn't *see* it," Connor broke in. "I'm telling you, she followed us here. She was just waiting for a chance to play a trick on you. Don't fall for it!"

I sighed. Connor's explanation did make sense.

"I guess," I agreed at last.

We kept walking. We were almost at the cemetery gate when I heard running footsteps behind us.

"Wait!" Luana called. "If you help me, maybe there is something I can do for you in return."

I spun to face her. Enough of this weird girl!

"Like what?" I sneered.

Connor folded his arms. "Yeah. Like what?"

"I have powers," Luana said breathlessly. "I learned many things when I sneaked into the sorcerer's library. Things that you might be interested in."

"Look," I started. "This all sounds very interesting, but—"

She kept talking. "I can change rocks into water. I can make it rain. I can turn things invisible. I can make a dog fly—"

"Yeah, sure!" I laughed. Even *I* could tell now that Luana was lying. No way could she do all that stuff! "Hey, I know. I've been wishing I was invisible all day. If you're so powerful, make me invisible!"

Luana shrugged. "Fine. I'll do it. It's easy!"

She sounded so sure of herself! For a second I felt shaken. Could she really do it?

No way! The new Jack knew better, I reminded myself. The new Jack could take a joke. But he wouldn't be fooled.

"Okay, Luana," I challenged. "We're ready. Make us both invisible. Me and Connor."

"All right," Luana said calmly.

She raised her face up to the sky and closed her eyes. I could see her lips moving quickly. But no words came out.

Her face was so serious. Again I felt that little thrill of doubt.

Was it possible? Could she really make us invisible?

Connor leaned over. "She's some kind of nut," he

whispered in my ear. "I think she really believes she's magic! Let's get out of here." He pulled the rusty iron cemetery gate open.

Luana's eyes snapped open. "By morning you will be invisible. But only from sunup to sundown. Remember that."

Connor was already through the gate.

"Whatever you say," I told Luana quickly. "Uh—thanks!"

I sprinted to catch up to Connor.

"She was too weird," I said when I caught up with him.

"Yeah," Connor agreed. "Talk about a freak show."

But in the back of my mind, I couldn't help wondering.

Maybe, just maybe. . . .

That night, the phone rang as I was clearing the dinner dishes off the table.

My older sister Carrie answered. When I came out of the kitchen, she tossed the cordless at me. "It's your loser friend, Connor."

"So—invisible yet?" he teased when I picked the phone up.

"Yeah, right. Remember—it's not supposed to happen until sunup," I joked back. "But I'm ready, man."

We talked for a few minutes, but then I hung up because Carrie kept bugging me to get off the phone.

After I cleaned up, I watched my favorite show on TV and did my homework. Then I went to bed.

As I lay there in the dark, I sighed. Even though I didn't really believe Luana could do it, I still wished I could really be invisible tomorrow. After the horrible day I had, I didn't know how I could ever show my face at school again.

I picked up my lucky spider ring, which was sitting on my night table. I slipped it on, so I wouldn't forget to wear it in the morning. "You better bring me better luck tomorrow," I whispered.

The alarm clock startled me the next morning. I rubbed the sleep out of my eyes and unwrapped myself from my sheets.

The floor felt cold on my bare feet. I shoved my feet into my slippers and stumbled down the hall.

As I approached the bathroom, I heard Carrie's alarm go off. I locked the bathroom door so she couldn't barge in.

Then I peered blearily into the mirror.

Huh? Something was wrong.

I rubbed my eyes again. And again.

Hey! Where was I?

I had no reflection!

None!
I stared down at myself.
Nothing there. No feet. No arms. Nothing.
I brought my hand up to my face.
It couldn't be.
But it was.
I was invisible!

About R.L. Stine

R.L. Stine is the best-selling author in America. He has written more than one hundred scary books for young people, all of them bestsellers.

His series include *Fear Street, Ghosts of Fear Street* and the *Fear Street Sagas.*

Bob grew up in Columbus, Ohio. Today he lives in New York City with his wife, Jane, his teenage son, Matt, and his dog, Nadine.

R·L·STINE

Is The Roller Coaster Really Haunted?

THE BEAST

❏ 88055-1/$3.99

It Was An Awsome Ride—Through Time!

THE BEAST 2

❏ 52951-X/$3.99

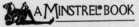

A MINSTREL® BOOK

Published by Pocket Books

Simon & Schuster Mail Order Dept. BWB
200 Old Tappan Rd., Old Tappan, N.J. 07675

Please send me the books I have checked above. I am enclosing $_____ (please add $0.75 to cover the postage and handling for each order. Please add appropriate sales tax). Send check or money order--no cash or C.O.D.'s please. Allow up to six weeks for delivery. For purchase over $10.00 you may use VISA: card number, expiration date and customer signature must be included.

Name _____

Address _____

City _____ State/Zip _____

VISA Card # _____ Exp.Date _____

Signature _____ 1163

SIMON & SCHUSTER
AUDIO

Simon & Schuster A Viacom Company

R·L·STINE'S
GHOSTS OF FEAR STREET ®

HALLOWEEN BUGS ME!

Simon & Schuster Audio presents another terrifying tale for kids from R.L. Stine's *Ghosts of Fear Street* series! Featuring an all-star cast of readers, special spooky tattoos inside, and the chance to collect and save points for fun *Fear Street* stuff, *Halloween Bugs Me!* is another frighteningly fun audiobook from the people who brought you *Three Evil Wishes*, *The Creature from Club Lagoona*, and *Why I'm Not Afraid of Ghosts*. Listen...if you dare!

❏ **HALLOWEEN BUGS ME!**
R.L. STINE'S GHOSTS OF FEAR STREET® AUDIOBOOK
1 Hour/1 Cassette
$7.95/$9.99 Can.
0-671-52133-0

Simon & Schuster Mail Order Dept. BWB
200 Old Tappan Rd., Old Tappan, N.J. 07675

Please send me the audiobook I have checked above. I am enclosing $_____ (please add $0.75 to cover the postage and handling for each order. Please add appropriate sales tax). Send check or money order—no cash or C.O.D.'s please. Allow up to six weeks for delivery. For purchase over $10.00 you may use VISA: card number, expiration date and customer signature must be included.

Name _____

Address _____

City _____ State/Zip _____

VISA Card # _____ Exp.Date _____

Signature _____ 1420

EAU CLAIRE DISTRICT LIBRARY

R·L·STINE'S

GHOSTS OF FEAR STREET ®

1 HIDE AND SHRIEK	52941-2 / $3.99
2 WHO'S BEEN SLEEPING IN MY GRAVE?	52942-0 / $3.99
3 THE ATTACK OF THE AQUA APES	52943-9 / $3.99
4 NIGHTMARE IN 3-D	52944-7 / $3.99
5 STAY AWAY FROM THE TREE HOUSE	52945-5 / $3.99
6 EYE OF THE FORTUNETELLER	52946-3 / $3.99
7 FRIGHT KNIGHT	52947-1 / $3.99
8 THE OOZE	52948-X / $3.99
9 REVENGE OF THE SHADOW PEOPLE	52949-8 / $3.99
10 THE BUGMAN LIVES!	52950-1 / $3.99
11 THE BOY WHO ATE FEAR STREET	00183-3 / $3.99
12 NIGHT OF THE WERECAT	00184-1 / $3.99
13 HOW TO BE A VAMPIRE	00185-X / $3.99
14 BODY SWITCHERS FROM OUTER SPACE	00186-8 / $3.99
15 FRIGHT CHRISTMAS	00187-6 / $3.99
16 DON'T EVER GET SICK AT GRANNY'S	00188-4 / $3.99
17 HOUSE OF A THOUSAND SCREAMS	00190-6 / $3.99
18 CAMP FEAR GHOULS	00191-4 / $3.99
19 THREE EVIL WISHES	00189-2 / $3.99
20 SPELL OF THE SCREAMING JOKERS	00192-2 / $3.99
21 THE CREATURE FROM CLUB LAGOONA	00850-1 / $3.99
22 FIELD OF SCREAMS	00851-X / $3.99
23 WHY I'M NOT AFRAID OF GHOSTS	00852-8 / $3.99
24 MONSTER DOG	00853-6 / $3.99
25 HALLOWEEN BUGS ME	00854-4 / $3.99

Available from Minstrel® Books
Published by Pocket Books

POCKET B O O K S

Simon & Schuster Mail Order Dept. BWB
200 Old Tappan Rd., Old Tappan, N.J. 07675

Please send me the books I have checked above. I am enclosing $_____(please add $0.75 to cover the postage and handling for each order. Please add appropriate sales tax). Send check or money order--no cash or C.O.D.'s please. Allow up to six weeks for delivery. For purchase over $10.00 you may use VISA: card number, expiration date and customer signature must be included.

Name _____

Address _____

City _____ State/Zip _____

VISA Card # _____ Exp.Date _____

Signature _____ 1146-23